FAMILY PETS

OUR PET FISH

by Michele Jakubowski
illustrated by Kev Payne

GRASSHOPPER

Tools for Parents & Teachers

Grasshopper Books enhance imagination and introduce the earliest readers to fiction with fun storylines and illustrations. The easy-to-read text supports early reading experiences with repetitive sentence patterns and sight words.

Before Reading

- Look at the cover illustration. What do readers see? What do they think the book will be about?
- Look at the picture glossary together. Sound out the words. Ask readers to identify the first letter of each vocabulary word.

Read the Book

- "Walk" through the book, reading to or along with the reader. Point to the illustrations as you read.

After Reading

- Review the picture glossary again. Ask readers to locate the words in the text.
- Ask the reader: What do Maya and Skipper both like to do?

Grasshopper Books are published by Jump!
5357 Penn Avenue South
Minneapolis, MN 55419
www.jumplibrary.com

Library of Congress Cataloging-in-Publication Data

Names: Jakubowski, Michele, author.
Payne, Kev, 1978- illustrator.
Title: Our pet fish / by Michele Jakubowski;
illustrated by Kev Payne.
Description: Minneapolis, MN: Jump!, Inc., [2022]
Series: Family pets
Includes reading tips and supplementary back matter.
Audience: Ages 5-7.
Identifiers: LCCN 2020058537 (print)
LCCN 2020058538 (ebook)
ISBN 9781636902012 (hardcover)
ISBN 9781636902029 (paperback)
ISBN 9781636902036 (ebook)
Subjects: LCSH: Readers (Primary)
Aquarium fishes–Juvenile fiction.
Classification: LCC PE1119.2 .J353 2022 (print)
LCC PE1119.2 (ebook)
DDC 428.6/2–dc23
LC record available at https://lccn.loc.gov/2020058537
LC ebook record available at https://lccn.loc.gov/2020058538

Editor: Eliza Leahy
Direction and Layout: Anna Peterson
Illustrator: Kev Payne

Printed in the United States of America at
Corporate Graphics in North Mankato, Minnesota.

Table of Contents

Bringing Skipper Home 4

Let's Review! 16

Picture Glossary 16

Bringing Skipper Home

Today, I get to pick out a pet fish!

"I want that one!" I say.
"I like his blue scales."

“What will you name him, Maya?” Dad asks.

“Skipper!” I say.

I can’t wait to set up his tank!

I put plants in Skipper's tank.

Skipper swims behind the plants.

We play hide-and-seek.

I feed Skipper every day.

"Just a pinch," says Mom.

Once a week, we clean Skipper's tank.

We use a net to take him out.

He is hard to catch!

It is time for my swimming class.

"I love to swim," I tell Skipper. "Just like you! See you later!"

Let's Review!

What color are Skipper's scales?

A. yellow **B.** blue **C.** red **D.** purple

Picture Glossary

net
An object with a handle and a pouch made from a grid of threads so water can flow through.

pinch
A small amount of something.

scales
Thin, flat, overlapping pieces of hard skin that cover the bodies of fish.

tank
A container in which fish and other water animals and plants can live.

Let's Review! Answer Key: **B.** blue